KU-166-531

BEST-LOVED
FAIRYTALES

hinkler

Published by Hinkler Books Pty Ltd
45–55 Fairchild Street
Heatherton Victoria 3202 Australia
www.hinkler.com.au

hinkler

© Hinkler Books Pty Ltd 2008, 2011

Illustrators: Melissa Webb, Anton Petrov, Omar Aranda,
Suzie Byrne, Mirela Tufan and Dean Jones
Prepress: Graphic Print Group
Typesetting: Graphicraft Limited

Images © Shutterstock.com: Seamless wallpaper pattern © Ozerina Anna;
Oval gold picture frame © Nodff.

All rights reserved. No part of this publication may be reproduced, stored
in a retrieval system, or transmitted in any way or by any means, electronic,
mechanical, photocopying, recording or otherwise, without the prior written
permission of Hinkler Books Pty Ltd.

ISBN: 978 1 7418 5017 8

Printed and bound in China

Contents

Beauty
and the
Beast

There was once a rich merchant who had three sons and three daughters. He spared no expense to give his children the best of everything. His daughters were beautiful, but the youngest was the loveliest. Everyone called her 'Beauty', which made her sisters very jealous.

The two oldest sisters were very proud and refused many offers of marriage because they were waiting for a duke or an earl to ask them. Beauty also refused several offers of marriage, saying she was too young and wished to stay with her father.

Then one day tragedy struck. The merchant's fine house burned down, with all their possessions. Then he discovered that his agents in distant countries had been cheating him out of his earnings. Finally, a great storm wiped out his fleet of ships, which were carrying the last of his goods to market. The merchant's fortune was destroyed.

All that was left was a small house in the country in the middle of a dark forest. The merchant told his children that they must move there and work for their living. The two eldest daughters thought that their fine friends in the city would take them in, but these friends forsook them in their poverty.

When they came to the house, the merchant and his sons worked the land to support them. Beauty rose at four every morning and worked, cooking, spinning and cleaning. She grew stronger and more beautiful than ever and remained cheerful for her father.

But her two sisters rose at ten and spent the day lamenting the loss of their fine clothes and friends. 'Look at our sister,' they said. 'She's such a stupid creature that she's happy with our dismal situation.'

The family had been living there for a year when the merchant received a letter. One of his ships with a rich cargo, which he had thought lost in the storm, had arrived safely to port.

The two oldest sisters were convinced that their poverty was over. They begged their father to bring back new gowns, jewels, ribbons and other trifles. The merchant begged them to be prudent, as he wasn't sure if this cargo was enough to discharge his debts, let alone set up a new fortune. Beauty alone asked for nothing. Her father, noticing her silence, asked her, 'And what shall I bring you, Beauty?'

'I only wish for your safe return, father,' she replied.

Her father was pleased but told her that she should have some pretty present and she should choose something.

'Dear father, if you insist, bring me a rose,' replied Beauty. 'I have not seen one since we arrived here and I love them so much.'

The good merchant set out to town, but when he arrived, it was as he'd feared. After a great deal of trouble, the merchant was left with little more than he had started with. He made his way home, thinking how much he wished to see his children again.

The merchant was still several hours from home as he made his way through a forest. As it grew dark, the wind howled and it started snowing heavily. The merchant realised that he was lost. He heard wolves howling and his clothes were soaked through. Suddenly, he saw a light gleaming through some trees.

As he made his way down a rough track towards the light, the merchant realised that the road was becoming easier. He came out of the forest into an avenue of trees ending at a splendid, illuminated castle.

The merchant made his way to the castle courtyard, but he was surprised to see no one about. However, he saw the stable door was open and went in, finding hay and oats laid out for his horse. The merchant went up to the castle door and entered. He walked through several splendid rooms before he found himself in a large hall with a good fire and a table set out with a feast for one person. He sat in front of the fire to warm himself and waited for the master of the house or some servants to appear, and he soon fell asleep.

The merchant woke when the clock struck eleven but still no one had come. Unable to contain his awful hunger, the merchant ate until he could eat no more. Growing braver, he made his way through more rooms until he found a chamber with a magnificent bed in it. Exhausted, he shut the door and went to sleep.

The next morning, the merchant awoke and discovered a suit of clothes laid out for him. 'Certainly, this place must belong to some fairy,' he thought, amazed.

The merchant looked out the window and saw the most beautiful gardens filled with lovely flowers, and not a trace of snow to be seen. He returned to the great hall and found breakfast laid out. 'Thank you, good fairy,' he said aloud, and then ate his breakfast.

After he had eaten, the merchant made his way outside to find the stables, but passing a rose arbour, he remembered Beauty's request. He gathered one to take to her, but then he heard an awful noise behind him. When the merchant turned around, he saw a frightful beast coming towards him and he fell to his knees.

'Ungrateful wretch!' said the Beast in a terrible voice. 'I saved your life, fed you and warmed you, and you repay me by stealing my roses, which I value above anything else in the world! You shall die for it!'

The merchant cried, 'Oh, please forgive me noble sir! I had no intention to offend. I was gathering a rose to take to my daughter, who asked me to bring her one.'

'Save your flattery!' growled the Beast. 'I am a beast, and I despise compliments!'

In despair, the merchant told the Beast of his misfortunes, why he was travelling in the forest and how Beauty had requested a rose.

The Beast listened, and then said, 'I will forgive you on one condition. You will give me one of your daughters. She must come here willingly. If one of them is brave and loves you enough, it will save your life. I will give you a month to see if any of them will return here. If not, you must come back here. And don't think you can hide, for I shall fetch you.'

The merchant reluctantly agreed. The Beast told him he must stay another night before he could leave. He did as the Beast instructed and found a meal prepared for him in the hall. The next morning, the merchant found another suit laid out for him. He breakfasted, then found his horse in the stables.

The merchant made his way home, where he was greeted by his children, who first thought his errand was a success due to his fine clothes. He handed Beauty her rose, saying to her, 'Here is your rose, although little do you know what it cost me.'

The children listened as their father told them what had happened and the two oldest daughters burst out crying. Beauty did not cry at all and the two sisters angrily accused her of causing their father's death.

'Why, our father will not suffer on my account,' replied Beauty. 'I caused the mischief, and since the Beast will accept one of his daughters, I will offer myself to him in our father's place.'

'Nay,' said the three brothers. 'We kill the monster, or perish.'

'Do not imagine you could do this,' replied their father. 'The Beast is strong. I am charmed by Beauty's offer but I will not allow it. I am old and have lived my life. I will go.'

'Then I shall follow you and take your place,' insisted Beauty. There was nothing anyone could say to persuade her otherwise

When the day arrived for her to go, she said goodbye to her brothers and sisters, but she did not cry. She and her father rode to the Beast's castle in the forest. Her father still tried to persuade her to return home but it was in vain.

When they arrived, the castle was lit up as before. In spite of her fear, Beauty could not help but admire the wonderful palace. They made their way into the great hall, where a feast for two awaited them. When they had finished eating, they heard a great roaring and then the Beast entered the hall. Beauty was terrified by his awful appearance but tried to hide it. When the Beast asked her if she had come willingly, she bravely replied, 'Yes.'

'I am pleased,' replied the Beast. Turning to the merchant, he said, 'You must leave at sunrise. Remember, you must never come here again.'

Turning to Beauty, the Beast said, 'Take your father into the next room and choose anything you wish for your father to take with him.'

Beauty and her father found two empty chests. The room was full of splendid dresses, ornaments, jewels and gold. The more they put in the chests, the more room there seemed to be, and they filled them so full that it seemed they'd need an elephant to carry them.

Beauty and her father then went to sleep and Beauty had a vivid dream. She saw a fine lady, who came to her and said, 'What you are doing will not go unrewarded. Be brave.' When Beauty awoke, she told her father the dream and it comforted him a little.

When the time came for the merchant to leave, they found two fine horses waiting in the courtyard carrying the heavy chests. Beauty did not cry until her father rode away. Then she sat in the great hall and wept, as she was sure the Beast would soon eat her.

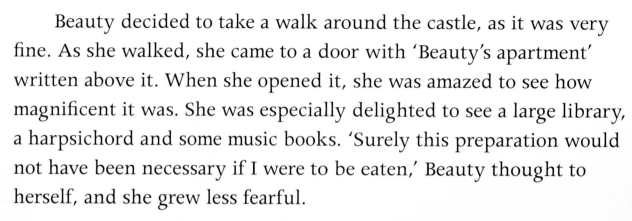

Beauty decided to take a walk around the castle, as it was very fine. As she walked, she came to a door with 'Beauty's apartment' written above it. When she opened it, she was amazed to see how magnificent it was. She was especially delighted to see a large library, a harpsichord and some music books. 'Surely this preparation would not have been necessary if I were to be eaten,' Beauty thought to herself, and she grew less fearful.

Beauty opened a book and on the first page, she read:

Welcome Beauty, do not fear,

You are mistress of all here.

Speak your wishes, state your will,

Swift obedience meets them still.

Alas,' sighed Beauty, 'all I want is to see my poor father.'

As soon as she spoke, a great mirror on the wall showed Beauty her father being met by her brothers and sisters. Her brothers looked sorrowful but her sisters could not contain their glee at the chests of treasure. The picture faded after a moment.

That night, as Beauty was sitting down to supper, she heard the Beast approaching. She was terrified, but the Beast asked, 'Will you allow me to join you for dinner?'

'As you please,' answered Beauty. Then the Beast asked her how she had spent her time and she told him about the rooms she found. When the Beast got up to leave after they had eaten, Beauty was surprised that an hour had passed. Maybe the Beast was not as terrible as she had supposed.

As he rose, the Beast asked, 'Beauty, will you marry me?'

Beauty was terrified she would anger him by refusing, but she answered, 'No, Beast.'

The Beast sighed and turned away, saying, 'Then good night Beauty.'

Welcome Beauty,
do not fear,
you are mistress
of all here.
Speak your wishes,
state your will,
swift obedience
meets them still.

When he had left, Beauty felt very sorry for the Beast. 'It is such a pity that someone so good natured should be so ugly.'

Beauty spent many months at the palace. Every day she found new surprises at the castle and every evening the Beast joined her for dinner and they talked for hours. Beauty got used to him and looked forward to his visits more than any other part of her day. She found the Beast was exceedingly kind and good-natured. The only worry was that every night as he left the table, the Beast asked her to marry him.

One day she said to him, 'Beast, I wish I could consent to marry you, as I see how my refusal saddens you. However, I am too sincere to make you think that might happen, but I love you as my greatest friend. Can you endeavour to be happy with that?'

'Alas, I love you with all my heart,' answered the Beast, 'but I must be happy with that, if you will promise to stay here always. Can you promise me that?'

Beauty hesitated, for that day in the mirror, she had seen her father, deathly ill from grief at her loss. 'I could promise, but I have such a desire to see my poor father that I might die if I can't,' she said.

'I would rather die myself than see you unhappy,' said the Beast. 'I will return you to your father and you will remain there and I shall die from grief.'

'No!' cried Beauty and she started to weep. 'I love you too much to be the cause of your death. Let me see my father for a month and then I shall return and stay with you forever!'

'You will be there tomorrow,' the Beast told her, 'but remember your promise. Take this ring. When it is time to return, twist it on your finger and say, "I wish to go back to my palace and see my Beast again." Sleep well Beauty and you shall soon see your father again.'

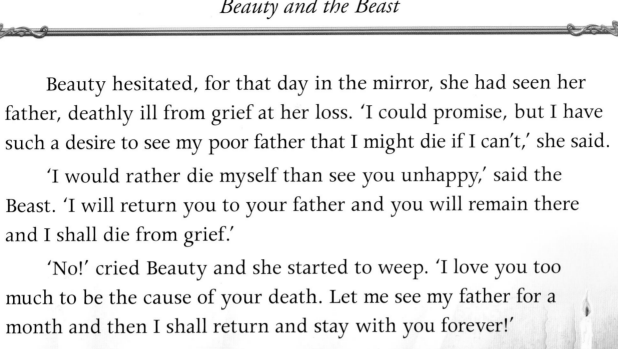

The next morning, Beauty awoke to find she was in a room in her father's house, along with a trunk filled with her clothes. She rushed to greet her father and her brothers and sisters. They were amazed to see her and asked her many questions. When they heard she was only there for a month, they lamented loudly.

As the month passed, Beauty found that nothing amused her and she found herself thinking of the palace and the Beast. When the month was over, her brothers begged her to stay a few days longer, as their father was recovering his health every day. Beauty missed the Beast, but she did not have the courage to say goodbye to her family just yet, and so, day after day, she put off her departure.

One night, she had a dream. She was wandering along a path in the palace gardens when she heard groans coming from behind some bushes. Pushing them apart, she found a cave entrance. Inside, she found the Beast stretched out on his side, dying. The fine lady from her first dream appeared and said to her, 'You are only just in time to save his life. This is what happens if people do not keep their promises!'

Beauty awoke in fright and discovered it was morning. She ran to her family and told them she must go back. That night, she said goodbye to her father and then twisted the ring on her finger, saying, 'I wish to go back to my palace and see my Beast again.' She immediately fell asleep. When she awoke the next day, she discovered she was back in her room in the palace.

Beauty put on one of her finest dresses and waited for dinner to see the Beast. But dinner time came and went and there was no sign of him. After waiting a long time, she ran through the palace trying to find him. She ran into the garden, looking for him, until she came to a path that she recognised from her dream.

Sure enough, behind some bushes was the cave, and stretched out on the ground was the Beast. Beauty ran to him and stroked his head, but he did not move or open his eyes. Crying, she ran to a fountain and fetched some water. When she sprinkled it on his head, the Beast opened his eyes.

'Oh, how you have frightened me!' she wept. 'I never knew how much I loved you until now, when I thought it was too late to tell you!'

'Can you really love something as ugly as me?' asked the Beast. 'Ah Beauty, I was dying because I thought you had forgotten me. Go to the palace and wait for me there.'

Beauty returned to the hall. The Beast came to her and sat with her to eat dinner. They talked about her visit to her family. When dinner was over, the Beast rose to leave, and then asked her, 'Beauty, will you marry me?'

'Yes, dear Beast,' she answered.

As she spoke, a blaze of light erupted outside. It seemed that fireworks were exploding outside and triumphant music was playing. Turning to the Beast to ask him what all this meant, she saw that the Beast had disappeared and in his place stood a handsome prince.

When she asked where the Beast was, the prince replied, 'You see him here. An evil witch cursed me to remain a beast until a beautiful maiden agreed to marry me without knowing who I really was. Only you were able love me for my goodness underneath my ugly form and I love you with all my heart.'

Then Beauty and the prince were transported to the prince's kingdom, where they were greeted by two stately ladies. Beauty recognised one from her dreams and the other was so grand that she must be the queen. The lady from her dreams, who was a good fairy, said, 'Queen, this is Beauty, who had the courage to rescue your son from his curse. Only your consent to their marriage is needed to make them perfectly happy.'

'I consent with all my heart!' cried the queen, and she embraced her son and Beauty. The fairy sent for Beauty's family and they joyfully arrived for the wedding, which was celebrated with the utmost splendour. Even her sisters were happy for Beauty and they all lived happily ever after.

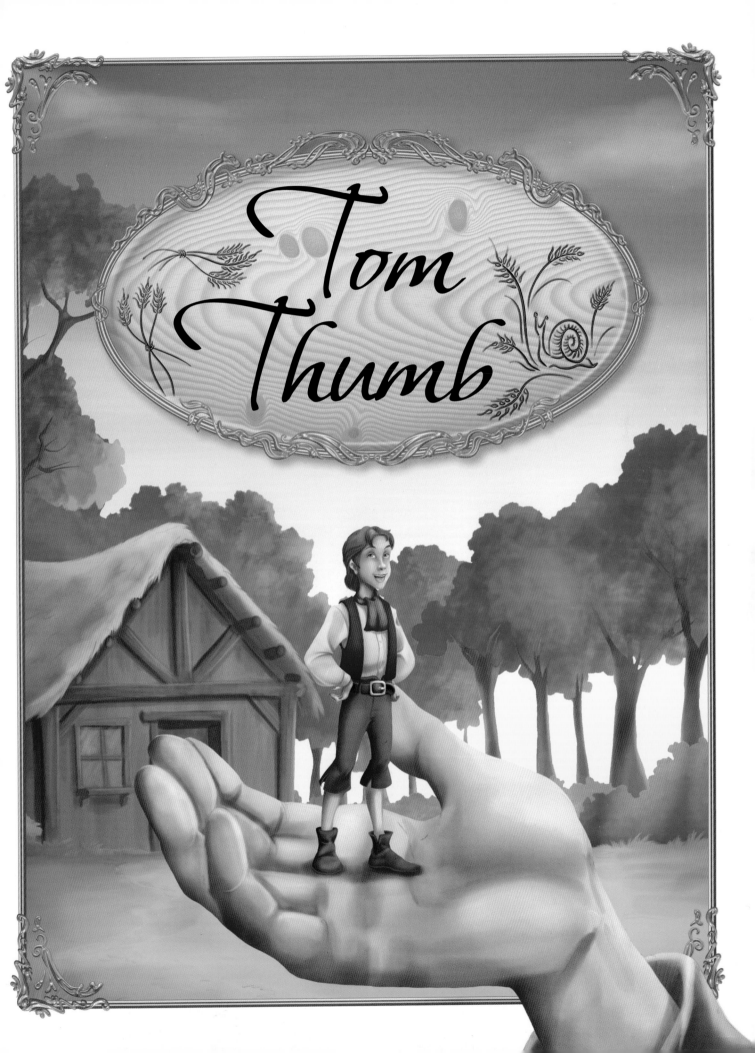

There once lived a poor woodsman and his wife. Every evening, the woodsman would sit next to the fire while his wife would spin at her spinning wheel.

One evening, the woodsman said to his wife, 'How lonely it is for just you and me to sit here by ourselves without any children to play about and amuse us. Other people's houses seem so happy and merry with their children and ours is so quiet.'

'How very true,' sighed his wife. 'How happy I should be if I had even one child! Even if it were as little as my thumb, I would still be very happy and love it dearly.'

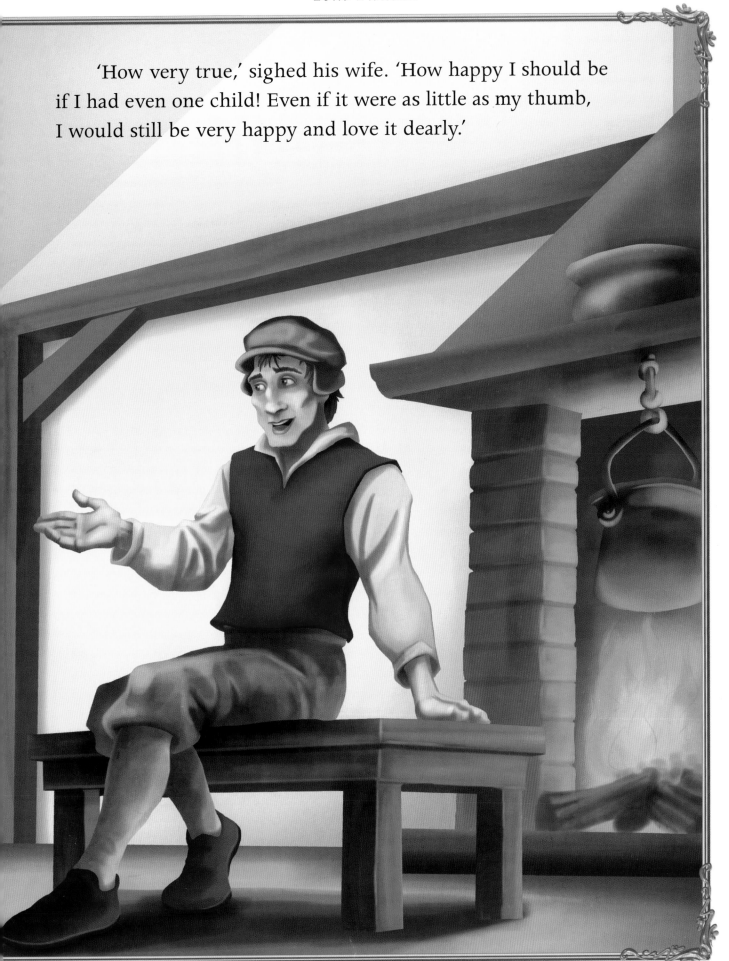

Now it came to pass that the good woman's wish was fulfilled, for not long after, she had a little boy. He was healthy and strong and perfect in every way, except he was no bigger than a thumb.

'He is just what we wished for,' said his parents, 'and we will love him very much.'

His parents named him Tom Thumb. They gave him plenty of food, yet despite all their efforts, he stayed the same size as he was when he was born. Still, his eyes were sharp and sparkling and he was clever and quick, so he succeeded in all that he did.

One day, his father was preparing to go into the forest to cut some wood. He was in a hurry and muttered, 'Oh, if only I had someone to bring the cart to meet me, for I need to hurry.'

'Oh Father,' cried Tom, 'I can bring the cart to you. It shall be in the woods by the time you need it.'

His father laughed kindly and said, 'Now Tom, how can you do that? You cannot reach the horse's reins.'

'Don't worry,' replied Tom. 'If Mother will only harness the horse to the cart, I will sit in the horse's ear and tell him which way to go.'

'Well,' replied his father, 'we will try it this once and see how it goes.'

When the time came, his mother harnessed the horse and set Tom in its ear. Little Tom cried out, 'Gee-up!' and 'Whoa!' and the horse went along just as well as if the woodsman himself was driving it.

Now it happened that as they were turning a corner and Tom was calling out, 'Gee-up!', two strangers came along. 'What an odd thing that is!' exclaimed one. 'There is a cart and the driver is calling to the horse, but he is nowhere to be seen!'

'That is very strange,' agreed the other stranger. 'Let's follow the cart and see where it goes.'

So the two men went on into the wood, following the cart. At last, the cart came to where the woodsman was cutting trees in the forest. When Tom saw his father, he called out, 'See Father, I am here with the cart all safe and sound! Now take me down.'

His father took hold of the horse's bridle with one hand and lifted Tom out of the horse's ear with the other hand and put him down on a tree stump, where Tom sat, happy as can be.

The two strangers were watching. They were struck dumb with wonder when they saw little Tom Thumb. Finally, one turned to the other and said, 'That little chap could make us a fortune if we were to show him in town for money! We must buy him.'

So they went up to the woodsman and asked, 'How much would you sell the little man for? He would be far better off with us than with you and we shall make sure he comes to no harm.'

'No indeed,' replied the woodsman. 'He is my own flesh and blood and he is dearer to me than all the silver and gold in the world.'

But Tom had heard what the men said. Climbing up his father's coat and perching himself on his shoulder, Tom whispered, 'Take the money, Father. It will do you and Mother a great deal of good and I shall return to you soon.'

After a great deal of persuasion from the two men, the woodsman agreed to let Tom go with them.

'Where would you like to sit?' asked one of the men.

'Oh, put me on the brim of your hat,' replied Tom. 'I can walk about and view the country and I'll be in no danger of falling off.'

So they did as he asked and paid the woodsman his gold. When Tom had said farewell to his father, they set off.

They walked and walked until the sun started to set. Then Tom said, 'Let me down, as I am tired.'

The strangers were not happy about letting Tom down and it was with some difficulty that he finally persuaded them. Finally, the man took off his hat and set Tom down in a ploughed field next to the road.

Tom immediately ran off into the field along a furrow. He ran and ran, and just as he was about to be seized by one of the men, he slipped into an old mouse hole.

'Good night sirs!' Tom cried out loudly. 'I'm off! You can go home without me!'

The men cursed and raged at Tom. They found a sharp stick and poked it into the hole, but it was in vain. Tom just crawled further until the stick could not reach him. At last it grew dark. The men were forced to go on their way without their prize, angry as can be.

When Tom was sure they had left, he crept out of the hole. He tried to cross the ploughed field but the furrows were so high that he was in danger of falling down in the dark and breaking his neck. At last, he came across a large empty snail shell.

'How lucky,' Tom thought. 'I can sleep here safely through the night and then make my way when the sun comes up.'

Tom crept inside the shell and settled himself down. But as he was falling asleep, he heard some more men pass by the field. There were two of them and they were talking to each other.

'How shall we rob the rich old parson of his gold and silver?' one said to the other.

'I can tell you how!' Tom cried out at the top of his voice.

'What was that?' said one of the thieves, startled. 'I'm sure I heard someone speak!'

The two thieves stood listening and Tom spoke again. 'Take me with you,' he said, 'and I shall show you how to get the good parson's money!'

'Where are you?' asked the confused thieves, looking around.

Tom crawled out of the snail shell and replied, 'Look down to the ground and you will see where I am.'

The two thieves found him and picked him up. 'You little elf!' they exclaimed. 'What could you do for us?'

'Why, I can easily sneak between the iron bars over the windows of the parson's house,' replied Tom. 'I can pass you whatever you would like.'

'That's a good idea,' said the thieves. 'Come along and let's see what you can do.'

When they came to the parson's house, Tom slipped through the window bars into the main room. Then he cried out at the top of his voice, 'Will you take all that is here?'

The two thieves were frightened and whispered back to him, 'Speak more softly! Be quiet, so you don't wake anybody!'

But Tom acted as though he didn't understand them. Again, he cried out loudly, 'What would you like me to take? Shall I throw it out the window to you?'

Tom shouted so loudly that the maid, who was sleeping in the next room, woke up. She raised herself up on her elbow, listening.

The two thieves had run off a short distance in fear, but at last they plucked up their courage and crept back, thinking that Tom must be playing a joke on them.

They whispered softly to Tom, 'Now let us have no more of your pranks and pass out some of the money.'

Then Tom called out as loud as he could, 'Very well! Hold out your hands and I will give it all to you!'

At this, the maid sprang out of bed and ran to open the door. The two thieves ran off as though a wolf were at their tails. The maid looked into the room but couldn't see anything in the dark, so she went off to get a lamp.

By the time the maid returned, Tom had slipped out the window into the barn. She looked everywhere, searching every hole and corner. Finding nobody, she went back to bed, thinking it was a dream.

Tom crawled into the hay loft and found a snug place to sleep. He lay down, meaning to sleep until daylight and then find his way home to his parents. But what other troubles would befall him!

The maid got out of bed at dawn to feed the cows. Going straight to the hay loft, she picked up a bundle of hay. It happened to be the very heap on which Tom Thumb lay fast asleep. He slept on until he awoke with a start and found himself in the mouth of a cow, which had eaten him along with the hay!

Tom soon realised where he was and had to have all his wits about him to avoid the cow's teeth. At last he was swallowed by the cow and ended up in her stomach. 'It is very dark!' he exclaimed. 'They forgot to build windows in here!'

Tom tried to make the best of his bad luck but he did not like his new quarters at all. More and more hay kept coming in and the space left for him grew smaller and smaller. At last, he cried out as loudly as he could, 'No more hay! No more hay for me!'

The maid happened to be milking the cow. She heard someone speak but saw no one. Sure it was the same voice she'd heard the night before, the maid was so frightened that she fell off her milking stool. She picked herself up out of the dirt and ran to get the parson.

'Sir, sir! The cow is talking!' she exclaimed.

'Surely you are mad!' said the parson. But he went with her to see what the matter was.

They had barely entered the barn when Tom called out, 'Don't bring me any more hay!'

Then the parson was also frightened. Thinking the cow was bewitched, he ordered his man to kill it. The cow's stomach was thrown on to the dung heap with Tom still lying inside.

Tom set about trying to climb out of the stomach through the hay, which was not an easy task. At last, just as he was about to get his head out, more bad luck befell him. A hungry wolf jumped out and swallowed the stomach in one gulp, with Tom still inside. The wolf ran into the woods.

Despite this, Tom was not disheartened. Thinking the wolf would not mind having a chat as he went along, Tom called out, 'My friend, I can show you where you can get a splendid meal!'

'Where is it to be had?' asked the surprised wolf.

'I can show you a house,' said Tom, and he described his own home. 'Crawl through the drain into the kitchen. There you will find the pantry full of cakes, ham, beef, bacon, chicken and everything that you could wish for.'

The wolf did not need to be told twice. That night, he went to Tom's house and squeezed in through the drain into the kitchen. There he feasted to his heart's content. When the wolf had eaten all that he could, he tried to squeeze his way out through the drain. But he had eaten so much that he could not fit through to get out.

This was what Tom had reckoned on. Now he began to make a great noise, singing as loudly as he could.

'Would you be quiet?' said the wolf. 'You will wake everybody in the house up!'

'Look here!' cried Tom. 'You've had your fun and now it's my turn!' Again he began to sing at the top of his voice.

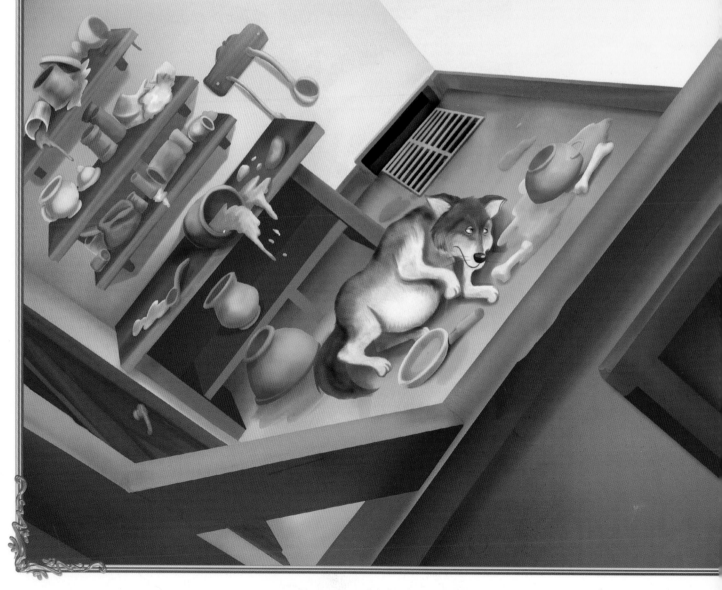

The Musicians of Bremen

A farmer once owned an old donkey. The donkey had worked faithfully for his master for many years. He'd carried huge sacks of wheat up the hill to the mill and bags of flour back down again, pulled heavily laden carts great distances and been ridden into town and back by the farmer's wife and children.

As he grew older, the poor donkey's strength began to fail him and he was no longer able to perform all the tasks that the farmer set him. With each day that passed, the donkey became more and more unfit for the hard work for which the farmer needed him.

At last, the farmer decided that it was time for him to get rid of the poor old donkey, as he could not afford to keep the beast if he could not perform his duties. However, the old donkey overheard the farmer talking to his wife about whether he should turn the donkey out or put an end to him. The donkey, guessing that his future at the farm looked grim, decided he would run away.

After some thought, the donkey resolved that he would take the road to the town of Bremen, famous for its freedom, where he could make his own living as a town musician. So off he headed down the road to that great city.

After the donkey had walked for a little way, he came across a dog lying down next to the road. The dog was panting as though he was tired after running a long distance.

'Hello friend,' said the donkey. 'Why are you panting and so out of breath?'

'Alas!' replied the dog. 'Now that I'm old and getting weaker all the time, my master has decided that I can no longer make myself useful when he's hunting. He decided get rid of me, but I escaped and ran away. I've been travelling such a long way, but I have no idea how I am going to earn my livelihood.'

'I've got an idea,' said the donkey. 'My master was also going to get rid of me because I was getting too old to work for him. I have also run away and I am making my way to Bremen, where I will become a town musician. Why don't you join me and we shall earn our living by making music together?'

The dog happily agreed, and so the two animals continued down the road together, talking about their plans to become musicians.

After the donkey and the dog had gone a little further, they spied a cat sitting by the road, looking as miserable as a cat could possibly look.

'Hello dear lady,' said the donkey. 'Why do you look so very sad?'

'You'd look miserable too if you were in danger of being thrown in the well,' replied the cat. 'Now that I am getting old, my teeth and claws are becoming blunt. I'd much prefer to lie by the kitchen fire and purr and sleep instead of running about the house chasing mice all day. My mistress was going to get rid of me because I was of no further use to her, so I ran away. But now I don't know what is going to become of me.'

'Why don't you come with us to Bremen?' suggested the donkey. 'The dog and I have also run away from our masters because we are too old and so we are going to try earning our way by becoming town musicians. You are bound to be an excellent night-time singer!'

The cat was very pleased with this idea and so the three animals continued down the road together towards Bremen.

The donkey, dog and cat had walked a little further when they saw a rooster perched on a farm gate. He was loudly crowing with all his might, creating an enormous racket.

'Bravo!' cried the donkey. 'What a wonderful performance! But tell me, why are you making all this fuss?'

'I have been a good rooster and foretold fine weather for wash-day,' said the rooster, 'but instead of getting any thanks, I heard that my mistress has company coming for Sunday lunch. She has told the cook to cut off my head tomorrow and cook me in a soup for them to eat! So here I am, crowing with all my might while I still can.'

'Goodness me!' exclaimed the donkey. 'You had better come along with us, good sir. Anything would be better than staying to have your head removed! Who knows? If we can all sing in tune, your powerful voice will be a very pleasing addition to our performance.'

The rooster was very happy to accept this offer and so he joined them on their travels to Bremen. The four animals went on down the road together, quite jolly.

However, as they went along, the four friends realised that they could not reach Bremen in one day. As night approached, the travellers came to a wood. They talked together and decided that they would spend the night in the woods and then continue on to Bremen the next morning.

The donkey and the dog lay down to sleep on the ground under a great tree. The cat climbed up into the branches of the tree for her rest. The rooster flew up to the top of the tree, as that was the safest place for him to perch for the night.

As was his habit, the rooster looked around on all sides to make sure all was well before he settled down to sleep. As he was looking out into the wood, the rooster spied a little light off through the trees, bright and shining.

'I see a light!' the rooster called down to his friends. 'There must be a house nearby, as the light does not seem very far away!'

'If that is so,' said the donkey, 'it would be best if we got up and investigated. After all, this wood is not the best place to sleep, especially when there is somewhere close by that might be much better! They might have a nice warm stable and some fresh hay for me to munch on.'

'I wouldn't mind a bone or two either, or a bit of meat to eat,' said the dog.

'Maybe there's a cosy basket by the fire and a piece of fish to dine on,' said the cat.

'Or a snug hen house with some tasty corn for me to peck at,' said the rooster.

So the four friends decided they would seek out better quarters for the night. They set off together into the woods towards where the rooster had seen the light.

As they came closer, the light shone brighter and brighter until they could see a snug little house, all lit up. Now, it turned out that this was a house in which a gang of fearsome robbers lived.

The donkey, being the tallest, went up to the window and peeked in. 'Well, donkey, what do you see?' asked the dog.

'What do I see? I see a large table laid out with all kinds of splendid things to eat,' replied the donkey. 'I also see a gang of robbers sitting around the table, eating and drinking and looking very comfortable.'

'That sounds like it would be very suitable for us,' said the rooster.

'Yes indeed,' said the donkey. 'Now if only we could get in there.'

The four friends consulted together on the best way to get the robbers out of the house. After a great deal of discussion, they hit on a plan.

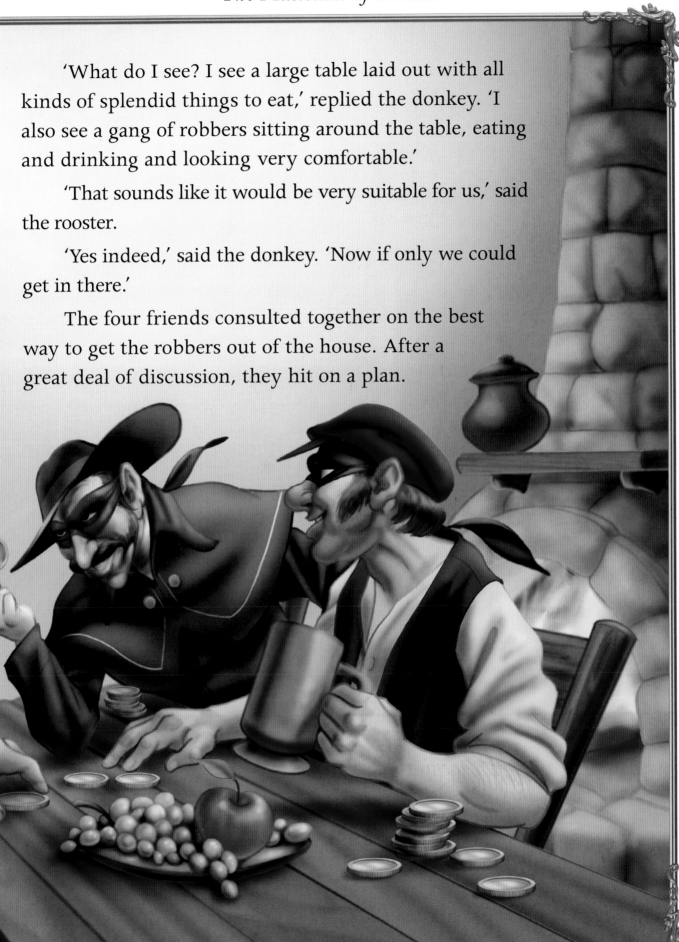

The donkey stood up on his hind legs with his front legs resting on the window sill for support. The dog climbed up on to the donkey's back and then the cat scrambled up on to the dog's shoulders. Finally, the rooster flew up and perched himself on top of the cat's head.

When they were all ready, the donkey gave a signal and the animals began to perform their music. The donkey brayed loudly, the dog barked furiously, the cat meowed at the top of her voice and the rooster crowed deafeningly.

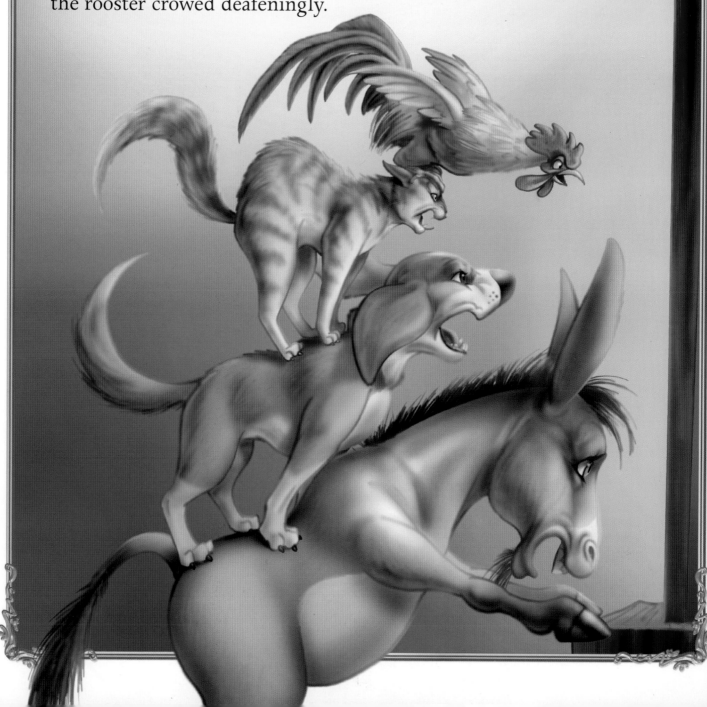

Then, the four animals crashed in through the window, tumbling amongst the broken glass with a hideous clatter! The robbers, who had already been alarmed by the noisy performance, thought some terrible goblin must be after them, and they all took to their heels and fled into the woods.

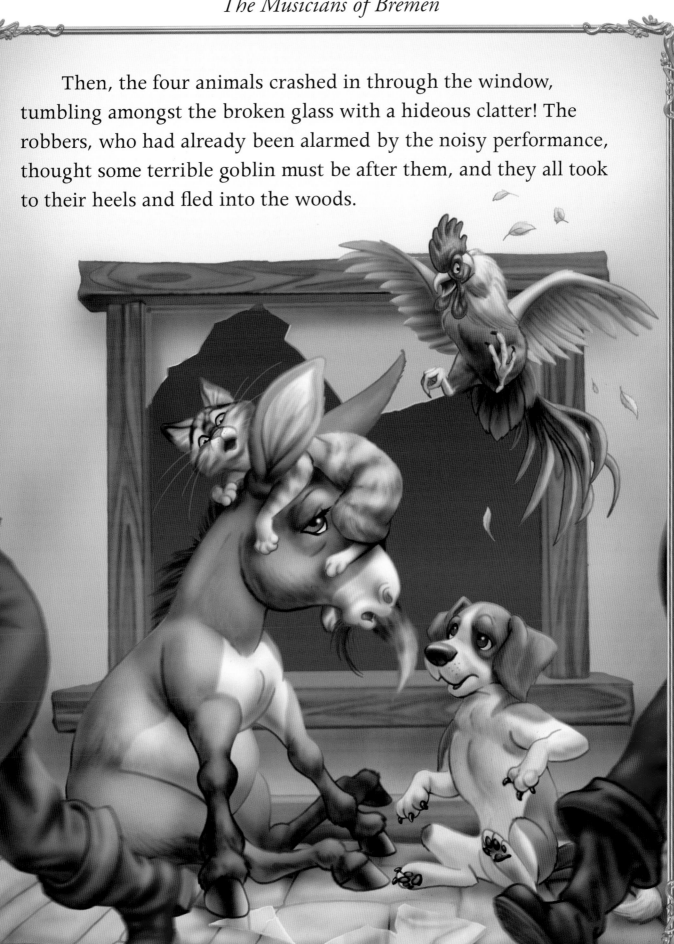

Once the coast was clear, the four friends sat down at the table and finished the robbers' splendid meal, feasting as if they hadn't seen food for a month.

When they had finished their meal, they put out the lights and each found a place to sleep. The donkey lay down outside in the yard on a pile of straw; the dog stretched out on a mat behind the front door; the cat curled up on the hearth in front of the ashes of the fire; and the rooster settled himself down on a beam in the ceiling. They soon fell asleep, as they were very tired from their long journey.

As midnight drew near, the robbers, who were watching from afar, saw that no light was burning in their cottage. As it all seemed quiet and still, they thought that maybe they had been in too much of a hurry to run away. The captain, worried that they'd left their lair for no reason, instructed one of the thieves to go back to the cottage and investigate.

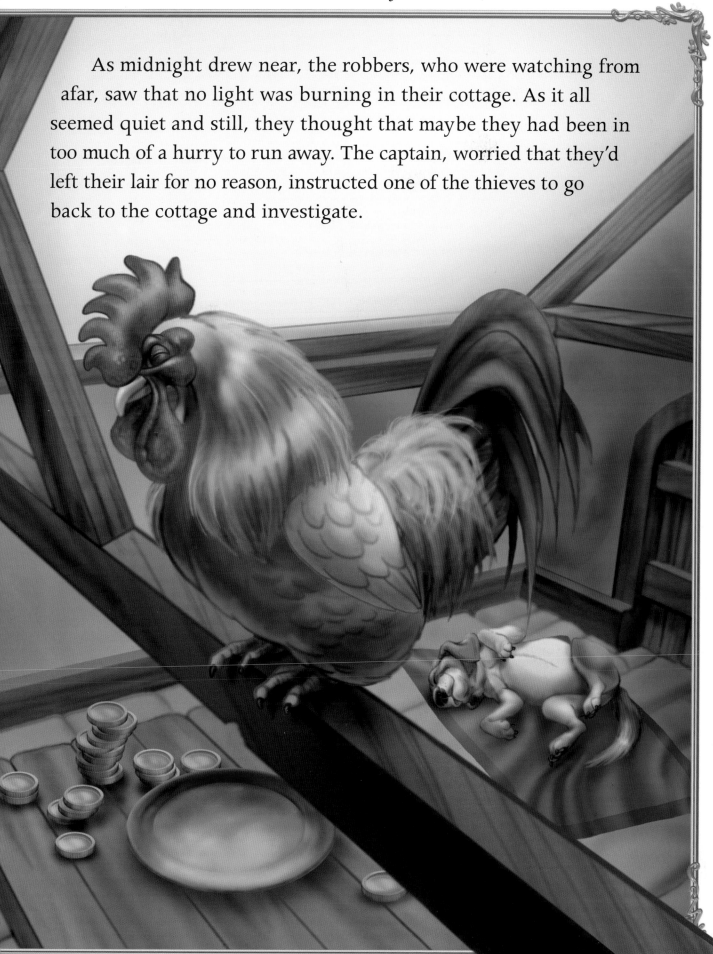

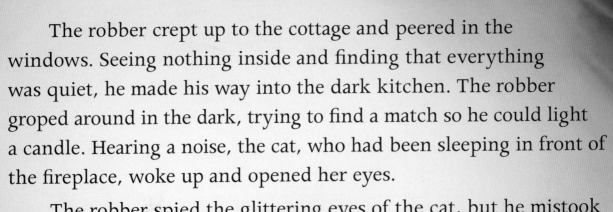

The robber crept up to the cottage and peered in the windows. Seeing nothing inside and finding that everything was quiet, he made his way into the dark kitchen. The robber groped around in the dark, trying to find a match so he could light a candle. Hearing a noise, the cat, who had been sleeping in front of the fireplace, woke up and opened her eyes.

The robber spied the glittering eyes of the cat, but he mistook them for burning coals in the fireplace. He stumbled forward, holding out the match to try and light it with the coals, but he only succeeded in poking the poor cat in the face. At once, the cat flew into a rage and jumped up, spitting and scratching the unfortunate robber in the face with her claws.

The frightened robber cried out in terror and ran to the front door, but he stumbled over the dog, who was woken by all the noise. At once, the dog jumped up, growling furiously and biting the robber's ankles and legs with his sharp teeth.

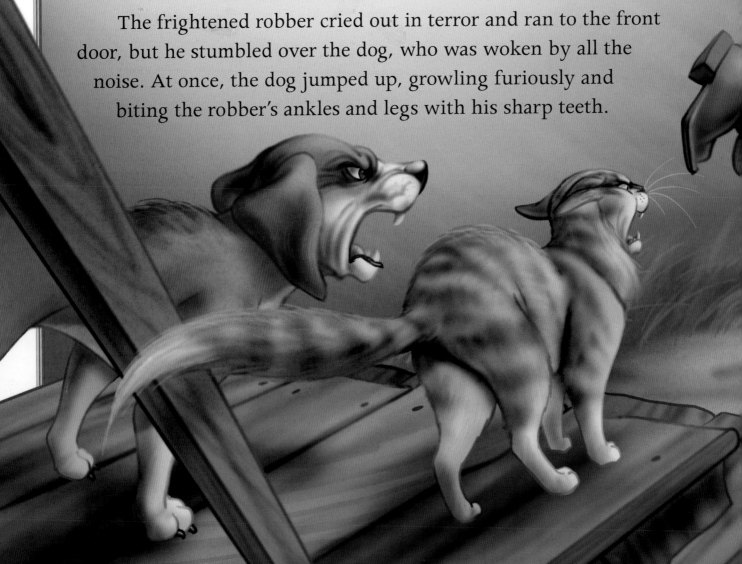

The ill-fated robber ran out the door into the yard, bumping into the donkey, who had got up to investigate what all the fuss was about. The donkey kicked out at the robber with his hind legs, catching the fellow squarely in his chest.

All this time, the rooster, who had also been awoken by the noise, stood in the rafters, crowing out 'Cock-a-doodle-doo!' at the top of his voice.

The robber ran back to his gang as fast as he could to make his report to the captain.

'It was awful!' the robber cried. 'I went into the kitchen, where I was attacked by a horrid witch who spat and scratched at me with her long sharp fingernails!"

The robber paused for breath before continuing.

'As I ran out of the house, I was attacked by a man standing behind the door who stabbed me in my leg with a sharp knife!' he said.

He paused to show his colleagues his bleeding leg.

'Then I fled out into the yard,' said the robber, 'where I ran into a huge black monster, who rose up in front of me and struck me with his huge, heavy club!'

The other gang members gasped as they looked at the robber's bruises.

'Finally, as I ran away, a devil cried out from the roof of the house. "Throw that rascal up to me!" it shrieked. I ran away as fast as I could and I'm never going back there!' the frightened robber finished.

From that time on, the robbers never dared to go back to the house. The four travellers were so pleased with their new quarters that they set up house there and never made it to Bremen. And there they are, it is said, until this very day.

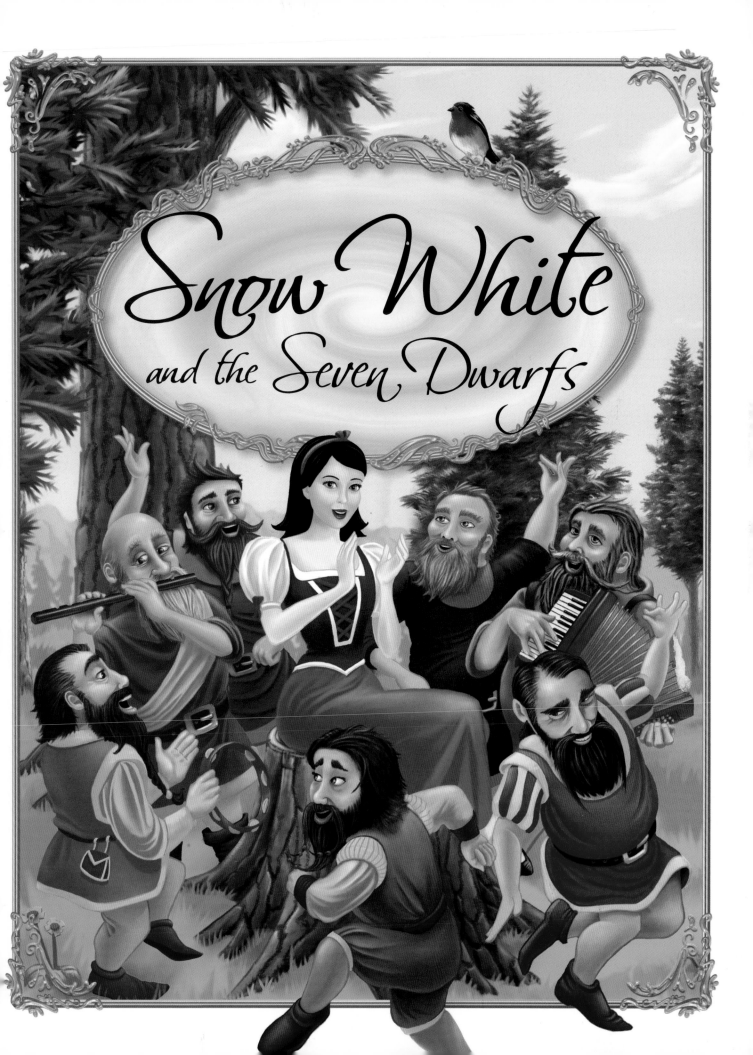

Once upon a time, in the middle of winter when the snowflakes were falling from the sky, a queen sat sewing at her window, which had a frame of black ebony wood. As she sewed, she looked out at the snow and accidentally pricked her finger with the needle. Three drops of blood fell from the open window into the snow.

As she looked at the brilliant red on the white snow, the queen thought to herself, 'If only I had a child with skin as white as snow, with lips as red as blood and hair as black as ebony.'

Soon after that, the queen had a little daughter. She was named Snow White, because her skin was as white as snow, her lips as red as blood and her hair as black as ebony. Alas, soon after the child was born, the queen died.

A year later, the king remarried. His new wife was a beautiful woman, but she was also proud and vain. She could not bear the thought that someone else might be more beautiful than her. She had a magic mirror which she looked into every morning, and asked:

'Mirror, mirror, on the wall,

Who in this land is the fairest of all?'

The mirror would always reply:

'You, Queen, are the fairest of all.'

The queen was always satisfied, because she knew that the mirror had to tell the truth.

As the years passed and Snow White grew up, she became more and more beautiful. Eventually, she was even more beautiful than the queen herself. One day, the queen asked her mirror:

'Mirror, mirror, on the wall,

Who in this land is the fairest of all?'

The mirror answered:

'You, my queen are fair, it's true,

But Snow White is a thousand times fairer than you.'

When the queen heard this, she turned white with fury and jealousy. From that time on, whenever the queen looked at Snow White, her heart heaved in her breast. So great was her hatred that she had no peace, day or night, and her envy and pride grew like a weed.

Finally, she summoned a huntsman and ordered, 'Take Snow White out into the woods. I never want to see her again. Kill her, and bring me her heart as proof she is dead!'

The huntsman took Snow White out into the woods. But when he drew his knife, Snow White begged him to spare her life. The huntsman took pity on her and could not bear to harm her. 'Run away, poor child,' he said to her.

'The wild animals will soon devour her,' the huntsman thought sadly, but he was relieved that he did not have to kill her. He spied a young boar in the forest and killed it, cut out its heart and took it back to the queen as proof of Snow White's death. The queen was very pleased.

Poor Snow White was all alone in the great forest. She looked around, and then she began to run. She ran over sharp stones and through thorn bushes and she saw wild animals, but she came to no harm.

Snow White ran for as long as she could, until it was almost evening. Then she saw a little cottage in the forest, so she went inside to rest. Everything in the cottage was very small but it was very neat and clean. There was a table set with seven places, all with little plates, mugs, spoons, knives and forks. A little loaf of bread sat on every plate and each little mug had some wine in it. Against the wall were seven little beds.

Snow White was so hungry and thirsty that she ate a piece of each loaf and drank some wine from each mug. After that, she tried all the beds, but some were too short and some were too hard, until she tried the seventh bed, which suited her very well. She lay down and fell asleep.

When it was dark outside, the owners of the cottage came home. They were seven dwarfs who dug and mined in the mountains for gold and silver. The dwarfs lit their seven candles and saw that someone had been in their house, for things had moved from where they left them.

The first cried, 'Who has been eating from my plate?'

The second cried, 'Who has been eating my bread?'

The third cried, 'Who has been sitting on my chair?'

The fourth cried, 'Who has been using my fork?'

The fifth cried, 'Who has been cutting with my knife?'

The sixth cried, 'Who has been meddling with my spoon?'

The seventh cried, 'Who has been drinking from my mug?'

Then the first dwarf looked around and exclaimed, 'Who has been lying on my bed?'

The other dwarfs all cried out that someone had been lying on their beds too. But the seventh dwarf saw Snow White asleep on his bed and called the others to come and see her. They looked at her by the light of their seven candles and exclaimed, 'Good heavens! What a lovely girl she is!' They didn't wake her up but let her sleep through the night.

The next morning, Snow White woke up and saw the seven dwarfs. She was frightened, but soon realised they were friendly and introduced herself. She told them how her stepmother tried to kill her but the huntsman had spared her life and she had run until she found their cottage.

The dwarfs said, 'If you will keep house for us, you can live here and we will take care of you.' Snow White agreed with all her heart.

Each day, the dwarfs went to work in the mountains, digging for gold and silver, while Snow White stayed home alone. The dwarfs warned her, 'The queen will soon discover where you are. Make sure you don't let anyone in.'

The queen believed Snow White was dead and that she was the most beautiful again. She went to her magic mirror and asked:

'Mirror, mirror, on the wall,

Who in this land is the fairest of all?'

The mirror answered:

'You, my queen are fair, it's true,

But Snow White, beyond the mountains, with the seven dwarfs,

Is still a thousand times fairer than you.'

This upset the queen, as she realised that Snow White was still alive. She couldn't bear the thought that someone was more beautiful than her, so she dressed herself up as an old peddler woman. In this disguise, she went to the house of the seven dwarfs and knocked at the door. She called out, 'Beautiful wares for sale!'

Snow White looked out the window and asked what was for sale. 'Fine laces in all colours!' replied the old peddler.

'She looks like an honest woman,' thought Snow White, and she opened the door. She bought a pretty bodice lace.

'Let me lace you up,' said the disguised queen, but she pulled so hard that Snow White could not breathe and she fell down as though she were dead.

'You used to be more beautiful,' laughed the queen, and went on her way.

Soon after, the seven dwarfs came home. When they saw poor Snow White lying there, they lifted her up and saw the tight lace. They quickly cut it and Snow White began to breathe again. When the dwarfs heard what happened, they said to Snow White, 'That old peddler woman was no other than the queen! Make sure you let no one in when you are alone.'

When she got home, the queen went to her magic mirror and asked:

'Mirror, mirror, on the wall,

Who in this land is the fairest of all?'

The mirror answered:

'You, my queen are fair, it's true,

But Snow White, beyond the mountains, with the seven dwarfs,

Is still a thousand times fairer than you.'

The queen was furious that Snow White was still alive. Using her witchcraft, she made a poisoned comb. She disguised herself as another old woman and went to the dwarfs' house. She knocked at the door and called out, 'Fine wares for sale!'

Snow White looked out the window and said, 'I am not to let anyone in.'

'Surely you can take a look,' replied the old woman, pulling out the poisoned comb. Snow White liked it so much that she agreed and opened the door. The old woman offered to comb her hair, but as soon as the comb touched her, Snow White fell down unconscious.

'Now you are finished!' cried the queen, and went on her way.

Soon the seven dwarfs came home and saw Snow White lying on the ground as though dead. They pulled the poison comb out of her hair and Snow White awoke and told them what happened. Again, they warned her not to open the door to anyone.

The queen went home and again asked her magic mirror:

'Mirror, mirror, on the wall,

Who in this land is the fairest of all?'

The mirror answered:

'You, my queen are fair, it's true,

But Snow White, beyond the mountains, with the seven dwarfs,

Is still a thousand times fairer than you.'

The queen flew into a rage. 'Snow White shall die!' she shouted.

She went to her secret room and made a poisoned apple. It had beautiful red cheeks and an alluring smell. Anyone would be tempted to eat it. Disguising herself as a peasant woman, the queen went to the house of the seven dwarfs and knocked at the door.

Snow White looked out the window. When she saw the peasant woman, she said, 'I am not to let anyone in.'

'I don't mind,' said the peasant woman. 'Don't worry, I will easily be able to sell my apples in time. In fact, let me give you this pretty one as a gift.'

'I cannot accept anything,' replied Snow White.

'What are you afraid of?' asked the peasant woman. 'Here, I'll cut it in two. You can eat one half and I shall have the other.'

The queen had cleverly made the apple so that only half was poisoned. She cut it in two and ate some of the unpoisoned half.

Snow White longed for the apple, and when she saw the peasant woman eating it, she could no longer resist. She took the apple and bit into it, but she barely had it in her mouth before she fell down dead.

'This time the dwarfs can't wake you!' the queen laughed.

The queen went home and asked the magic mirror:

'Mirror, mirror, on the wall,

Who in this land is the fairest of all?'

The mirror answered:

'You, Queen, are the fairest of all.'

And the queen was very pleased.

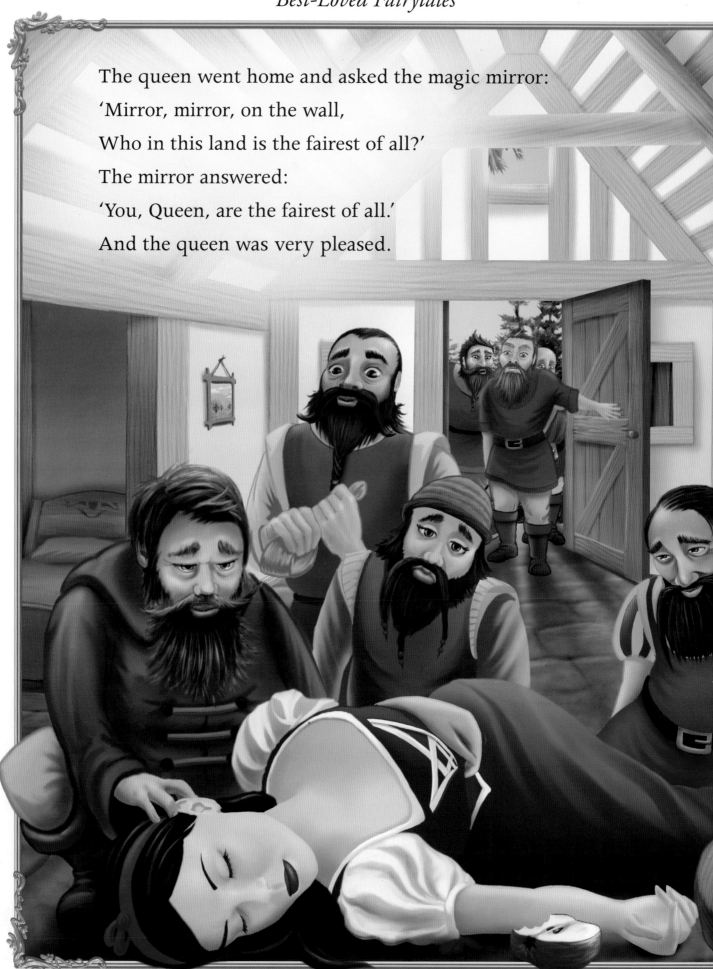

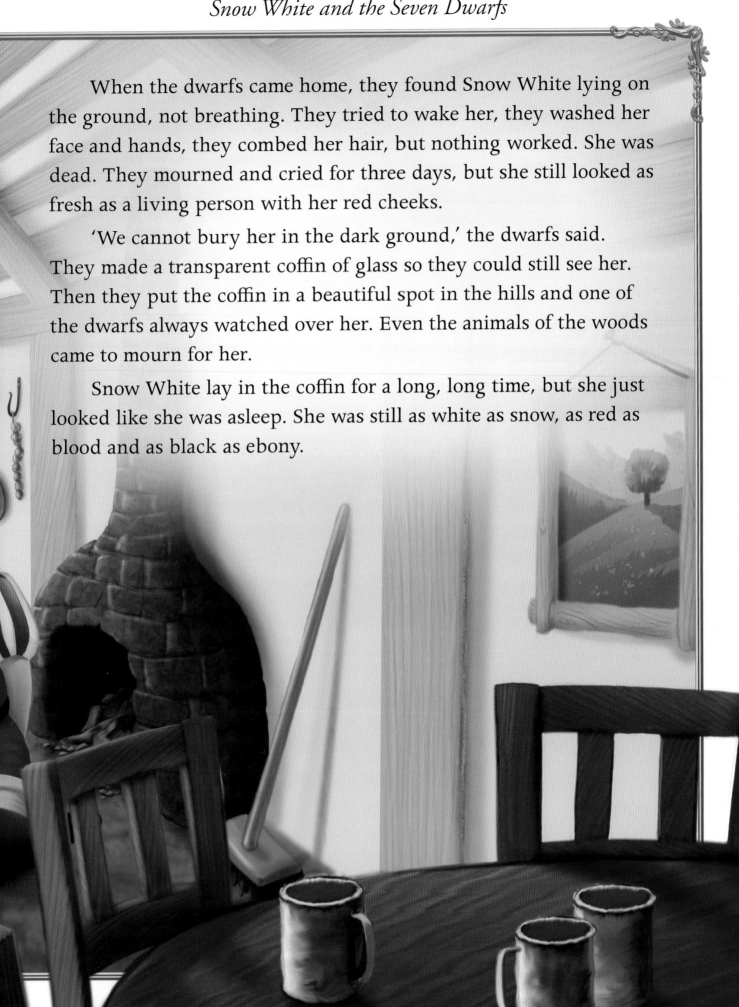

When the dwarfs came home, they found Snow White lying on the ground, not breathing. They tried to wake her, they washed her face and hands, they combed her hair, but nothing worked. She was dead. They mourned and cried for three days, but she still looked as fresh as a living person with her red cheeks.

'We cannot bury her in the dark ground,' the dwarfs said. They made a transparent coffin of glass so they could still see her. Then they put the coffin in a beautiful spot in the hills and one of the dwarfs always watched over her. Even the animals of the woods came to mourn for her.

Snow White lay in the coffin for a long, long time, but she just looked like she was asleep. She was still as white as snow, as red as blood and as black as ebony.

One day, a handsome prince entered the woods. He needed shelter for the night, and came to the dwarfs' cottage. He saw the coffin with Snow White in it. The prince immediately fell in love with Snow White, and begged the dwarfs to let him take the coffin. He offered them money, but the dwarfs said, 'We would not part with her for anything in the world.'

In despair, the prince said, 'Then please give the coffin to me. I cannot live without seeing her.'

Seeing his distress, the dwarfs took pity on him and gave him the coffin.

The moment the prince lifted the coffin to carry it home with him, the piece of poisoned apple was jolted out of Snow White's mouth and she awoke.

'Where am I?' Snow White asked.

The prince told her what had happened and said, 'I love you more than anything. Come with me to my father's castle and become my wife.'

Snow White saw the love in the prince's eyes and agreed. Their wedding was planned with great splendour.

Snow White's stepmother was invited to the prince's wedding.
After she put on her beautiful clothes, she asked the magic mirror:

'Mirror, mirror, on the wall,

Who in this land is the fairest of all?'

The mirror answered:

'You, my queen are fair, it's true,

But the young bride is a thousand times fairer than you.'

The queen was furious when she saw the bride was Snow White.
She died soon after, destroyed by her hatred and envy. Snow White
and the prince reigned happily for many years. They often visited the
dwarfs in the mountains, who had been so kind to Snow White in
her time of need.

Beauty and the Beast

Versions of the *Beauty and the Beast* story have been told for centuries. An ancient Roman myth called *Cupid and Psyche* features a beautiful maiden cursed by the goddess Venus to fall in love with a snake. However, Venus's son Cupid falls in love with Psyche and turns himself into the serpent, revealing himself as a young man at the end of the tale. The story of a beautiful girl caring for a beast, only to have him turn into a man, is found throughout many tales from Asia and Europe.

Other early European versions of the story include *The Pig King* by Italian Giovanni Straparola, published in *The Facetious Nights of Straparola* in 1550 with the beast as a pig, and the first version to be named *Beauty and the Beast*, written in 1650 by French aristocrat Marie-Catherine Le Jumel de Barneville and featuring a serpent beast.

In 1740, Madame Gabrielle-Suzanne Barbot de Gallon de Villeneuve wrote the first modern version of the tale. Her version of *Beauty and the Beast* was 362 pages long and featured fairies, kings and twelve brothers and sisters.

The version of *Beauty and the Beast* most familiar to modern readers was published 1756 by Madame Jeanne-Marie Le Prince de Beaumont, in a collection called *Magasin des enfants*. This version has the two jealous sisters marrying wealthy men, only to have unhappy marriages, while Beauty, who accepts the hideous but good Beast, ends up happy and content.

The Brothers Grimm recorded two stories featuring the original *Tom Thumb* character: *Thumbling* and *Thumbling's Travels*. The version presented in this collection is the original *Thumbling*.

In the sequel, *Thumbling's Travels*, Tom (or Thumbling) is carried up the chimney by the steam from the pot. He helps some robbers steal from the king's treasure chamber, is cooked into a black pudding and eventually eaten by a fox, who he convinces to let him go and rides back home. His father is so grateful that he allows the fox to eat his chickens.

It is thought that the folktale that the Brothers Grimm based their version on was the precursor to an English folktale of the same name. The English version combines the events of the two *Thumbling* stories and also mixes in many elements and characters of the King Arthur legends.

In the English version, the magician Merlin, disguised as a peasant, is given shelter by a childless couple. Out of gratitude, he casts a spell so that Tom Thumb is born. Tom ends up having many adventures, including a visit to fairyland, and he becomes an honorary Knight of the Round Table.

This story was recorded in verse by Richard Johnson in 1621. It was turned into a popular satirical play by the playwright Henry Fielding in 1730.

The Musicians of Bremen

The Brothers Grimm recorded *The Musicians of Bremen* in *Kinder- und Hausmärchen (Children's and Household Tales)*. It is the twenty-seventh story in their collection and was first included in the second edition, which was published in 1819.

In their introduction to the tale, the Brothers Grimm note that they found several versions of the story, including one in which the musicians don't drive out the robbers but peacefully join them for a meal and then entertain them. It is when the gang returns from thieving that they think they are being attacked, like in the Grimm's version.

The harbour town of Bremen is in northern Germany near the coast on the river Weser. In the story, the animals decide to head for Bremen because it is 'renowned for its freedom'. Bremen was a member city of the Hanseatic League, a wealthy trading guild that operated in the Baltic Sea. Towns of the League had no local nobles or aristocracy and owed their allegiance directly to the Holy Roman Emperor. Cities in the League could be found along the coast from France to Estonia.

Although the animals never made it to Bremen, there is a famous statue of the four friends perched on each other's backs in the town.

Snow White
and the Seven Dwarfs

The story of *Snow White* was told in many versions from Europe to Asia and Africa before the Brothers Grimm recorded it in *Kinder- und Hausmärchen* (*Children's and Household Tales*).

Some traditional versions of the story have Snow White rescued by robbers instead of dwarfs. Instead of a magic mirror, the step-mother converses with the sun or moon, or sometimes an animal.

Although it was included in the 1810 manuscript of their collection, the Brothers Grimm changed *Snow White* quite dramatically in the published edition. Initially, it was Snow White's own mother who tried to kill her, not her step-mother. Her mother takes her into the woods to gather flowers, then abandons her. At the end of the story, the king has his wife executed. It is thought this was changed by the Brothers Grimm to make the story more suitable for children.

In the final version of the Grimm's story, the evil step-mother eats the heart the hunter gives her as proof of Snow White's death. She also attends the wedding, where the prince forces her to dance wearing red-hot iron shoes until she falls down dead. Modern versions of the story have Snow White awakened with a kiss, instead of the apple jolting free from her mouth.